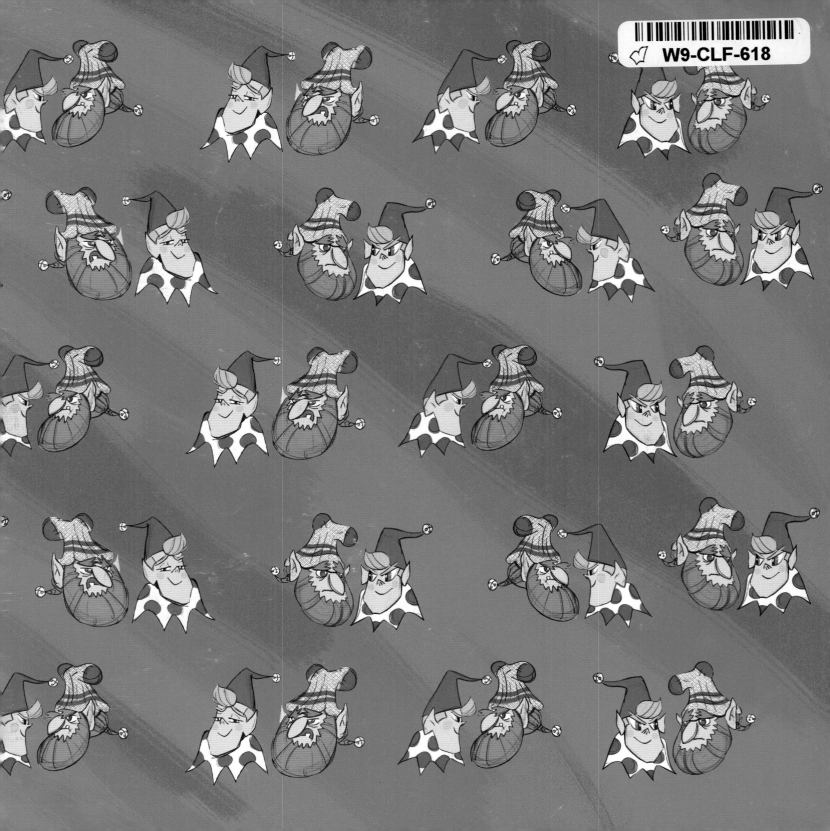

SQUARE
FISH

An Imprint of Macmillan

Square Fish books may be purchased for business or promotional use. For information on
bulk purchases, please contact the Macmillan Corporate and Premium Sales Department at
(800) 221-7945 x5442 or by e-mail at specialmarkets@macmillan.com.

Library of Congress Cataloging-in-Publication Data Available

ISBN: 978-1-250-04143-2

Book design by Patrick Collins

Square Fish logo designed by Filomena Tuosto

First Edition: 2013

1 3 5 7 9 10 8 6 4 2

mackids.com

The Dwarf in the Drawer

L. VAN KING

illustrated by CHUCK GONZALES

SQUARE FISH

NEW YORK

'Twasn't the night before anything, yet all through the land,
Parents were worried beyond their command.
Their children were nervous—they just could not rest,
For fears of NO GIFTS had them overly stressed.

That troublesome rascal, the shelven-bound elf,
Had twisted their heads since December the twelfth.

In a box he'd arrived,
With a smile quite contrived.
Oh, I knew in a snap—
There was mayhem on tap.

Who am I? you might ask.
Well, let me tell you the facts.

I'm the Dwarf in the Drawer,
And I lived here before . . .
Before that darn elf—
That insufferable bore!

I live in your drawer
With your clean underwear.
I play through the day,
And at night, watch Colbert!

Before that elf came, everything was in check.
No one got crazy, no one strained their neck
Trying to pick up that elf from under the couch.
You bet he's the reason that I'm such a grouch.

For most of the year, things at home were real peachy.

Then in came that usurper, acting all preachy.

Who died and made that elf king?

That creep who made Christmas a terrible thing?

I won't give you a list of impossible chores,
Like washing the lawn

Or mowing the floors.

Here is my mission—I'm willing to share:
YOU make my stories. YOU make me care.

I won't lead you astray, or down a dead end.
Don't call him your pal—he is not your friend.
And don't call after Christmas, when he goes away,
Packed up for the year in a box with a sleigh.

Knowing the difference
Between what's wrong and what's right?
You don't need elf intervention
To solve that tough plight.

Don't threaten
your brother

Or cheat
at Ping-Pong.

Don't eat all the cake—
You know that's all wrong.

But don't fret if your room is a messy pigsty.
Relax! I won't report you to the Big Guy.
I won't get uptight, or go on a rant.
Nope, HE is the snitch, that smug sycophant!

From my drawer, I read blogs and see all the posts.

But I'm here to tell you who loves you the most.

Not that strange creature, or even dear me.

It's those closest to you—your friends and family.

His elf magic will stray

If you touch him, they say.

But we all need some comfort: a cuddle, a hug.

So get rid of that guy, and warm up your mug . . .

As you melt in your armchair and read through these pages,
Here is a message for kids of all ages:
Don't believe in empty things like shelves or their elves.
You simply just have to believe in yourselves.

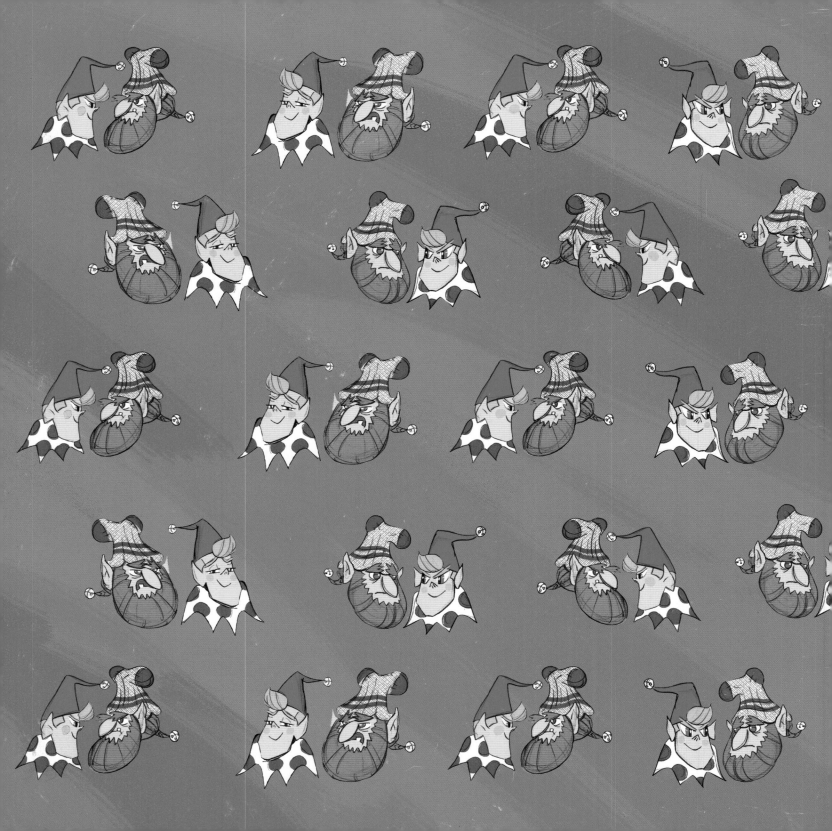